Canadian Cataloguing-in-Publication Data

Fraser, Ivan, 1945-
Peggy of the Cove: The Rescue of Peggy / Ivan Fraser
ISBN 0-9736872-1-5

I. Ivan Fraser Studio II. Title. III. Title: Rescue of Peggy.
PS8611.R38P44 2004   C813'.6   C2005-900364-2

1st printing January, 2005

Ivan Fraser (Publisher)

Ivan Fraser Studio
Peggy of the Cove ®
10236 Peggy's Cove Road
Glen Margaret, NS B3Z 3J1
902 823-2083   1 888 524-2252   fax 902 823-1757
ivanfraser@peggyscove.net   www.peggyscove.net

Cover Design – Brent Kowalczwyk – Crossbow International

Printed and bound in Canada by Friesens,
Altona, Manitoba, Canada R0G 0B0

Peggy of the Cove:
The Rescue of Peggy

by Ivan Fraser

Illustrated by
David Preston Smith

Excitement filled the air as our long voyage across the Atlantic Ocean was one day short of reaching Halifax, Nova Scotia. We had been blessed with perfect weather conditions during our trip. On this day, however, gentle evening breezes turned into strong gales with dark, angry clouds looming over the horizon. Waves grew bigger and bigger. All of the passengers were sent below.

Captain Smith, a hearty, experienced seaman, could be heard on deck shouting orders. Sailing through many storms, he always brought ship and crew safely to port. Everyone believed he would do the same this time as well.

Thick clouds continued to cover the moon and darken the waters. Everyone was unaware that just below the surface, Halibut Rock lay directly in their path. Without a lighthouse there was no warning to sailors of hidden danger.

Soon lightning flashed over the horizon with the sound of thunder rolling in the distance. Before long, the storm was directly overhead causing some passengers to pray for safety.

Giant waves pounded and washed over the ship. Captain Smith knew he must take shelter behind Shut-in Island at the entrance of St. Margaret's Bay. There they could wait out the storm.

All passengers were being shaken by the turbulent sea as they huddled below deck, and were holding onto anything they could, including each other. The constant tossing about made most passengers seasick.

Suddenly, the ship rose higher and higher as if climbing a steep mountain and for a split second seemed to stop. Then diving almost straight down, there was a deafening crash. The ship struck Halibut Rock.

A small girl surfaced, thrashing about in the swirling sea, desperately searching for something to hold onto. She was giving up hope when her hand grasped a rope with a small barrel attached. Holding on for dear life she prayed it would carry her safely ashore.

After being washed onto the rocks, the small girl wondered if she would survive. Finally strong arms lifted her fragile and shivering body to rescue from the ocean's cold and rocky coastline. She whispered a prayer of thanks as she saw the men holding a lifeline with her rescuer tied to its end.

Wrapping her in a wool blanket, the rescuer rushed the soaked and chilled little girl to the nearest house. Waiting ladies from the community changed her into dry clothes, happy that someone had survived such a terrible disaster.

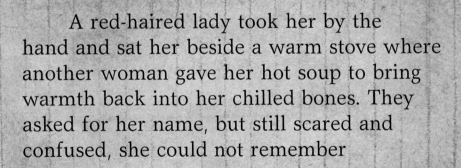

A red-haired lady took her by the hand and sat her beside a warm stove where another woman gave her hot soup to bring warmth back into her chilled bones. They asked for her name, but still scared and confused, she could not remember

Cozy, warm and tired, she dozed off. The man who rescued her, carried her upstairs and gently laid her on the bed. The red-haired lady tucked her in with warm blankets and gently brushed back the little girls locks of hair. She placed a tender kiss upon her forehead, while the child fell fast asleep.

After a time, the little girl awoke from a deep sleep. A soft, gentle hand stroked her face. "My name is Mary," she said, "Can you remember yours?"

"No I can't," She sobbed.

"That's all right, I'm sure it will come back. For now we'll call you Peggy so you'll know we are talking to you. Two years ago I had a little girl, Elizabeth, about your age who died of a fever. Her room is still like it was and will be yours if you come live with us. Would you like to be part of our family?"

She couldn't help but accept as a tear rolled down her cheek.

Mary took Peggy to her weathered home in this strange new land. They were inside only moments when three boys charged through the door. Mary introduced them as her sons, James, Peter and Joe. Then the door opened again, Mary said, "I would like you to meet my husband, John." Peggy stared in shock and disbelief; standing there smiling was the brave man who had rescued her.

Often Peggy climbed the rocks to gaze upon the sea and wonder about her past. Life had changed so suddenly. Her new family showered her with love, kindness and patience. Mary guided her through some difficult times. She helped build her faith and trust. With new hope, Peggy looked forward to an adventurous future living in the Cove...her new home.

Ivan Fraser is an established artist and photographer who was born and raised in Nova Scotia. His latest endeavors include writing a song, authoring books, and creating dolls and related products of the little girl who became know as "Peggy of the Cove" after being shipwrecked. It is his desire that *The Rescue of Peggy* touches your heart as you read about her life, from being shipwrecked to finding her new home, in the fishing village now know as Peggy's Cove.

David Preston Smith is recognized internationally as an Illustrator and Canadian Artist. His career was launched working on Aerospace Research projects initiated by NASA. Assignments have included illustrations for major corporations, publishers, film makers and he is currently illustrating books for children. He resides with his wife, Grace, overlooking the shores of St. Margarets Bay, Nova Scotia.